SHELBY & WATTS

Tide Pool Troubles

by ashlyn anstee

VIKING

CHAPTER 1

In the village of Valley Glen . . .

5

You know what that means.

A mystery to solve!

Shelby

fox

favorite book:
*Detective Dahlia
and the Sounds of Basketville*
favorite color: teal

Watts

badger

favorite book:
Encyclopedia of the World
(unabridged), 5th Edition
favorite color: maroon

The Case of the Missing Notebook

Clue 1: The spilled chamomile tea led to the chair . . .

Clue 2: Where I found a soft blanket, so I knew that's where you were sitting!

Clue 3: The bushes were rustled, as if something had disturbed them.

Deduction:
The book must have fallen off into the bushes when you accidentally fell asleep!

Solved!

Dear Shelby and Watts,

I'm sorry for writing you out of the blue, but I need your help.

My name is Fred and I'm a hermit crab.

My shell has become too small and I can't find a big enough shell to move into.

There isn't one ANYWHERE on the beach!

Shelby—Mary told me that you've read more mysteries than anyone she knows.

Watts—Mary said that you've read the whole encyclopedia cover to cover.

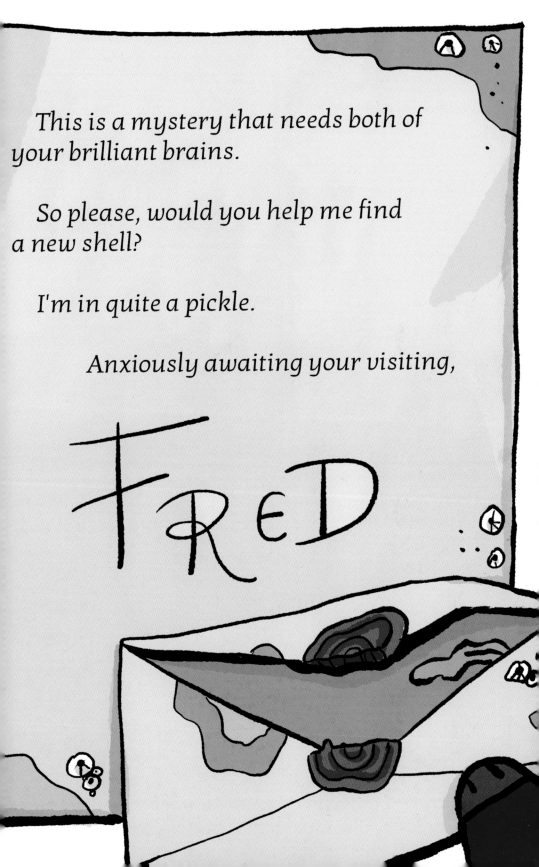

WATTS'S FUN FACTS

HERMIT CRABS LIVE IN SHELLS. THEY CHANGE THEIR SHELLS WHEN THEY OUTGROW THEIR OLD ONE!

A pickle? Why is he living in a pickle—

"In a pickle" means "in a difficult situation."

Do you think you can help?

Tweet!

It sounds like a mystery Detective Dahlia would solve.

I've always wanted to visit the seashore ecosystem.

Let's go!

Thanks.
I knew you two could help!

What are you bringing with you?!

Just a few essentials.

WATTS'S BAG

19

WATTS'S FUN FACTS

1/3 OF THE WORLD'S POPULATION
LIVES WITHIN 60 MILES (100 KM) OF AN OCEAN COAST!

CHAPTER 2

At the beach dunes . . .

Arty

rhinocerous

seaside collector
favorite color: green

Hmm ...
Come to think of it, no.

Maybe you should
look down the shore.
It's where the good shells are!

Thank you!

CHAPTER 3

Farther down the shore . . .

Cindy

seagull

favorite pastime: surfing waves
favorite color: sky blue

Have you seen a hermit crab named Fred?

Usually, the hermit crabs visit the shore looking for shells.

NOD

NOD

Fred

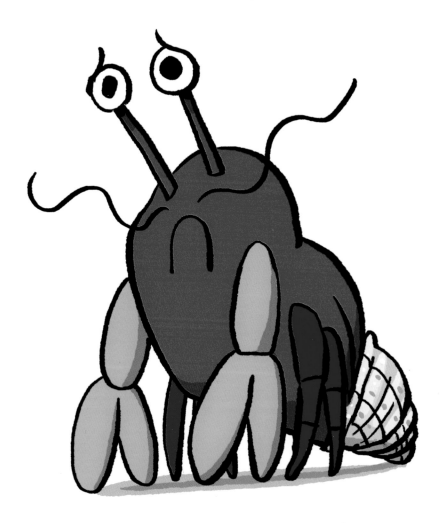

hermit crab

current mood: very squished
favorite color: red

44

CHAPTER 4

At the rocky tide pools . . .

LIFT

SARDINES

PACIFIC SARDINES CAN SWIM
IN SCHOOLS OF UP TO 10 MILLION FISH!

MUSSELS

MUSSELS FILTER-FEED FOR PLANKTON!
THEY CAN FILTER 17 GALLONS
OF WATER A DAY!

SEA
CUCUMBERS

SEA CUCUMBERS BREATHE THROUGH
THEIR BUTT!

oh my!

NUDIBRANCHS

NUDIBRANCHS COME IN A RAINBOW OF COLORS!
THEY GET THEIR GORGEOUS HUES FROM THE FOOD THEY EAT!

BARNACLES

BARNACLES BREATHE THROUGH FEATHERY LITTLE ARMS CALLED CIRRI!

STARFISH

STARFISH ARE NOT ACTUALLY FISH! MOST HAVE 5 LEGS, BUT SOME CAN HAVE UP TO 40 LEGS!

And . . .

LIFT!

Hello again!

What brings you back here?

I think you're mistaken! We've never met before.

HERMIT CRABS OFTEN LIVE
IN LARGE COLONIES OF 100 OR MORE!

CHAPTER 5

At the Field of Shells . . .

69

CHAPTER 6

The beach dunes . . .

The Case of the Missing Shells

Clue: Arty was eating chips,
which we later found at the shore.

Arty: seaside collector

Clue: Arty said he was looking
for sea treasures to collect.

CHAPTER 7

At the beach . . .

AN ECOSYSTEM: A COMPLEX COMMUNITY OF CREATURES AND THEIR ENVIRONMENT!

BEACH

FOREST

DESERT

ARCTIC

USES FOR SHELLS AROUND THE BEACH

FISH AND CRABS USE SHELLS
TO HIDE FROM PREDATORS!

ALGAE, SEA SPONGES, AND SEAGRASSES
WILL ATTACH TO SHELLS
AND LIVE ON THEM!

AND HERMIT CRABS
LIVE IN THEM!

THE SHUFFLE

AS HERMIT CRABS GROW, THEY NEED BIGGER SHELLS.

WHEN IT'S TIME TO MOVE INTO A LARGER SHELL.
HERMIT CRABS LINE UP FROM LARGEST TO SMALLEST
SO THAT THEY CAN TRADE UP!

EACH CRAB GETS A NEW SHELL!
NO WASTE, AND ROOM TO GROW!

THE BIGGEST SHELL GOES TO FRED, AND THEN
FRED'S SHELL GOES TO THE NEXT-BIGGEST CRAB . . .

UNTIL FINALLY EVEN THE SMALLEST CRAB
HAS A NEW SHELL TO GROW INTO.

Never take shells or other beach stuff from the beach, as they could be homes for hermit crabs and other ocean creatures. Even rocks can be homes to barnacles.

Take photos instead!

Eat seafood from sustainable sources! This helps prevent overfishing and preserves our oceans' delicate balance.

Leave the beach cleaner than when you found it. Take all human trash with you, while leaving the beach debris (kelp, logs, and organic matter) there on the beach.

(A bucket can build a great sandcastle, and can also help you carry trash home!)

Organize a beach clean-up day!

We can help!

For Grant—my partner in all things

VIKING
An imprint of Penguin Random House LLC, New York

First published in the United States of America by Viking,
an imprint of Penguin Random House LLC, 2021
First paperback edition published 2022

Visit us online at penguinrandomhouse.com.

Library of Congress Cataloging-in-Publication Data is available.

Paperback ISBN 9780593205334

Manufactured in China

1 3 5 7 9 10 8 6 4 2

TOPL

This book was drawn in Procreate and Photoshop on the iPad, with a few little
watercolor textures here and there.

Ashlyn Anstee grew up in a rainy city in Canada and then settled in a sunny city in the United States with her husband and four cats. She works in the animation industry, and in her spare time, drinks tea and takes naps. She writes, draws, illustrates, animates, and is the creator of the books *No, No, Gnome!*, *Are We There, Yeti?*, and *Hedgehog!*

Shelby & Watts: Tide Pool Troubles is her first graphic novel.